CORPUS MEMORIA: HAIR

A tangle of story

Avis Barlow

Unruly Press
An imprint of Literary Kitchen Press

This is autobiographical fiction. It is loosely based on the author's imperfect recollection of experiences over time mixed with factoids. Most names, characteristics, events, and dialogue are real, but some are not. Essential truth has been earnestly attempted but surely not attained.

Avisbarlow.com

Avis Barlow

ii

Hair
\ `her \

1: any of the fine threadlike strands
growing from the skin of humans,
mammals, and some other animals.
2: a very small quantity or extent.
3: exactly; right in every detail.

Avis Barlow

CONTENTS

Avis Barlow

In My Dream

There is a recurring dream pulling me under at night that leaves behind a film of vague unease. It is set in a meat locker where animals are brought by farmers, ranchers, and hunters after death for processing into parts, cuts, and sausage. Here, you feel the cold on the back of your hands. On your cheeks. You notice how the mist from your breath and the beads of water from the pipes encircling the room condense and fall heavily toward one of the many drains in the floor. The water and blood plus time have wearied the white and submarine-gray painted wall.

In late autumn, there are usually deer and pigs hanging, maybe a couple of steers. Some are already skinned. Blue tattoos or tags tell their stories of birth, place, and worth. But not in this shadowy place in between dark and dawn. Here, human parts fill the room. In the back, a few bodies hang on hooks, unskinned. Some have tattoos; some have tagged toes.

Behind one hanging body is a wall of hair of all colors, textures, and lengths. Some are on display on styrofoam and green-glass heads; others hang in skeins on a pegboard filled with hooks. In the center is a gilt frame holding three brooches woven with locks of brown and black hair pinned to a velvet-covered board.

For some of us, there are no boxes of journals we've been keeping since kindergarten or albums of family photos. Stories are tagged on our skin, our organs, our bones, and in our cells. Our minds have already been stripped clean.

While others sleep, I put on my coat and gloves and spend time in this meat locker. I pick up each part and put it up to my left ear to listen to the piles and piles of stories here. Stories queer people, women, and children have lived many times.

I listen to regain my own pieces and bear witness to each part's life. Some stories are loud enough to drown out what's alive outside my body. Some can barely be heard. At dawn, I put it back, find it a new home, or, more times than I usually admit, flush it away. I've learned that some stories need retelling so we don't forget; but some should only be heard once.

Corpus Memoria: Hair

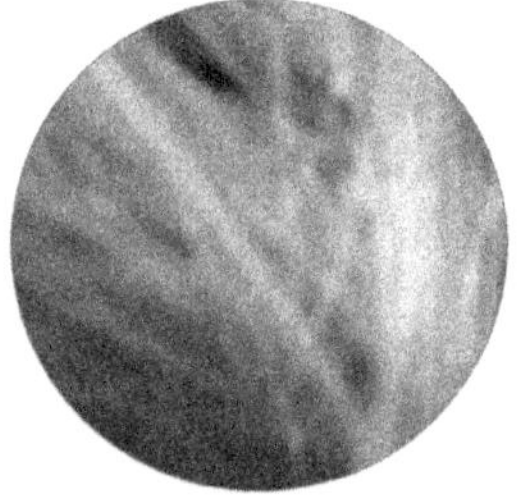

It is a myth that hair grows after death. The post-mortem contraction of skin and flesh causes the hair to protrude slightly. [1]

[1] https://www.almanac.com/fun-facts-and-myths-about-hair accessed 02/16/2024.

6

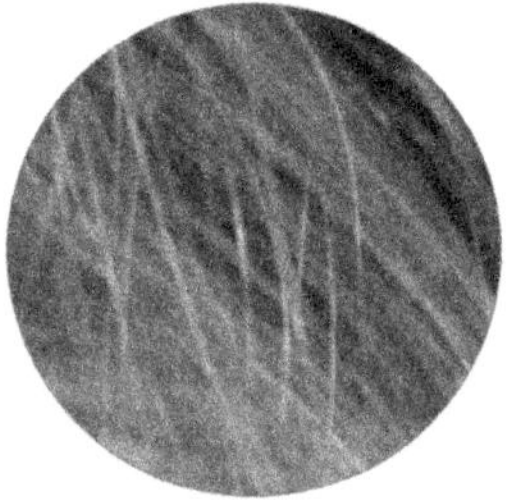

I Remember

I remember when queer spaces were in bars and clubs in industrial or non-residential neighborhoods with darkened windows, in public bathrooms, and in wooded city parks. You had to know they were there to know they were there. In the city in which I came of age, the old warehouse district — empty of deliveries and workers and activity at night — was the white gay and lesbian epicenter. Now, it is a city destination known for its expensive condos, shops, eateries, and exposed brick walls.

I cannot remember telling my best friends or telling anyone I knew. Except my mother. After the fact. In a lesbian bar. When I had a girlfriend of more than a few weeks to introduce. "I wish I was one," my mother said, leaning on the long wooden bar with a cigarette in her left hand and a scotch and water in the other. As if same-sex dating was somehow easier.

I remember when queers lived in neighborhoods near one another. In the

West Village, Boystown, Belmont Street, Castro, The Mission, and Dupont Circle. If you didn't know the bars, you knew where to be to meet someone who knew the bars or you could find the alternative papers listing the bars. If you were in college, you looked for gay dances, lectures by gays and lesbians, and student groups with a lot of women studies majors; I don't recall any events by or for the trans community.

I cannot remember why my roommate, Scott, tried to fix me up with the library sciences major he took class with. He pushed hard though. Had she seen me at a party? Or, had he taken me on as a newly out project? Scott died years ago of AIDS. I wish he was still here for many reasons: his twink flamboyance, love of costumes and adventures, and the charm he wielded to buffer the poverty that came from his eternal studenthood. Scott's storytelling skills came by way of Murfreesboro, Tennessee and were elaborate, hilarious, and just a little bitchy. He would make this sad, awkward story funny.

I remember not really fitting into any of the queer spaces or being particularly good at meeting women. I felt more comfortable with the men but could not understand why.

I cannot remember her name or anything I liked about her. I can only remember being repulsed by her over-cinched khaki pants, bad haircut, oxford shirts, and suburban pseudo-intellectual ways. She was a few years older but younger-seeming in her introverted world of books.

I remember cops writing down the license numbers of cars parked near the park where the gay pride rally was being held. Another pride event in a bigger city nearby was targeted by the Ku Klux Klan. We took a chartered school bus there and marched in the parade to spite them. Power in numbers! It was my first time talking to shirtless men with their nipples pierced and kissing my girlfriend during the day in public.

I cannot remember the details. I imagine it was at my apartment shared with three other roommates on the mattress on the floor: she still lived at home. She was unsure in moving from kissing to touching to clothes off. I had more confidence than made sense for my first time. After, I felt an urgency to get her back to her parents in their suburban home.

I remember when gay, straight, or lesbian seemed parallel. Trans was in its own orbit that seemed far away or abstract somehow. All was defined by who we fucked and how we presented ourselves publicly. We never spoke of how we identified inside. How our insides matched up with our lives in the outside world. It would take me decades to wonder about that.

I cannot remember saying much the next day to my roommates but do recall my meanness in talking about her and our one-night stand; covering up my inexperience with bitchiness. To prove I was queer enough to be there and not a straight hag hanger-on.

I remember when trans was a very performative manly-man and girly-girl extremist space. Getting confused that it was about clothes. There were lots of rules about what's enough and what's not. It felt very far away from me.

I cannot remember what Willa Cather book she gave me nor how I finally got her to stop calling or coming by under the guise of visiting Scott. I aped the rudeness of my gay friends' behavior after they tricked with someone vaguely regrettable.

I remember feeling something big shift into place when I first heard the word "nonbinary." Before then, I said bisexual but it never felt quite right. Now, I say queer. I cannot remember calling myself a lesbian, and lesbians never really saw me as one of them, unless they were drunk. How did they know? It took many years before I knew that too.

11

12

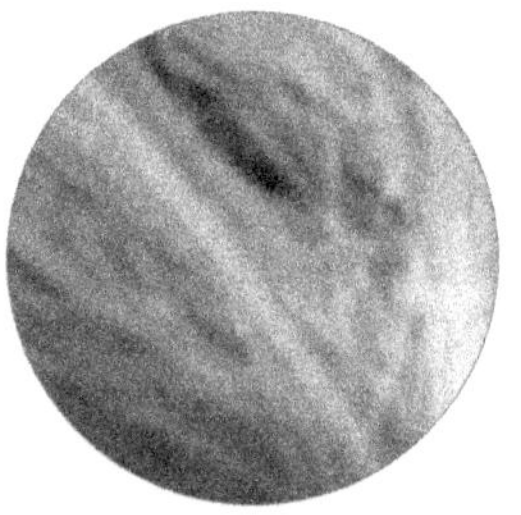

Most critics who acknowledge Cather's homosexuality see no traces in her fiction of what Lillian Faderman calls "same-sex love." According to Faderman, "perhaps she felt the need to be more reticent about love between women than even some of her patently heterosexual contemporaries because she bore a burden of guilt for what came to be labeled perversion." [2]

[2] Adams TD. My gay Antonia: the politics of Willa Cather's lesbianism. J Homosex. 1986 May;12(3-4):89-98. doi: 10.1300/J082v12n03_08. PMID: 3531325.

14

Cloaked

Date a woman named Lee.
The first one you'd notice in a room. A pink poetic creation that blooms for an audience. She'll sweep you up and a little later tell you that you're lucky to be with her.

> For a while, she'll be right.

Go.
Pack what you can carry in a garment bag and as many black garbage bags as you can carry. You have six hours to get away while she works. Take a taxi from the apartment you shared to Elena's; the long-haired work friend that you ate lunch with but never mentioned. The next morning, fly to a state she'll never guess to stay with a high school friend she never knew.

> Be free.

Act normally.
Tell her you are going to the library. Instead, ride the train up and down Twin Peaks. Get

yourself to a place she can't find. Imagine leaving. Later, ride up and down the hill while you plan the details of your escape. When you are ready, call in sick from the coffee shop around the corner and ride a bus from San Francisco to the airport. Find a place to sit until you feel brave enough to buy a ticket. It'll take awhile. Then, hide the ticket in the journal you carry everywhere. When you're ready, go home. Your excitement will fill the empty bus.

Don't let on.

Be sad.

Think of something sad. Maybe a time you were molested, humiliated, or overlooked in some tortured and painful way. Say, "I'm sad," until she looks up from her own concerns. Until she notices. Offers to make you cheap ramen with frozen mixed vegetables and egg. Be patient. When you're sad she doesn't get angry at you. Won't raise her voice. Won't cause you to pull one of her extensions out.

Neighbors will call the police.

Manage your location.

If her trucker ex-boyfriend, Carl, breaks into the apartment, lock yourself in the bathroom. He'll make sure you both know just how mad he is that she's dating a woman. After calling the police and getting him to leave, she'll tell you that it was no big deal. Don't believe her.

Never walk around unclothed.

Take an interest.
When she says, "I'm an artist," with confidence and regales you and everyone who shows the slightest interest with details from her community TV show, comics, poems, and many performances, write ARTIST in thick crayon or marker on a mirror and hold it up to her. Your arms might tire.

She won't notice.

Be very still.
If she tells you to lay your clothed body face down on the bed, do it. Let her straddle your lower back. So she can't see your face. So you are a captive audience to the story of what's been bothering her. So you can't move when she tells you she's been cheating on you. With Carl. Multiple times. And, with the well-oiled braided artist, Niama. Multiple times.

Movement will be startling.

Make no eye contact.
Look down or to the right. If asked a direct question, look her in both eyes and quietly pull her spirit toward yours. Hold your breath. Until she looks away.

Then, turn and go.

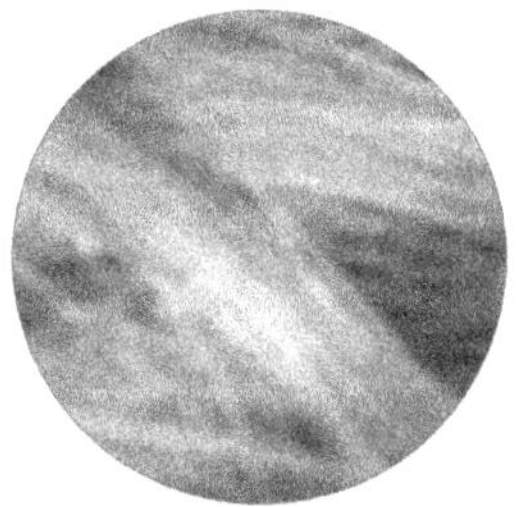

Ancient African communities believed that hair helped with divine communication. For this reason, hair styling was entrusted to close relatives. People thought that if a strand of your hair fell into enemy hands, you could be harmed. [3]

[3] https://www.africa.com/history-african-womens-hairstyles/ accessed 02/16/2024.

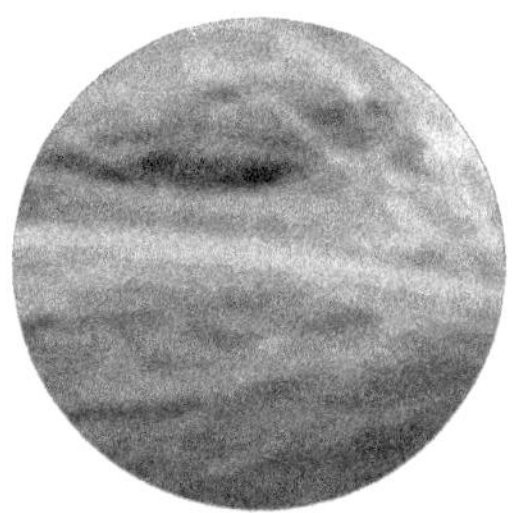

Everything is Fine

She is someone you would never see. An erased smudge in a crowd scene. Lightly present, she fears and hopes of being noticed. Pale in color and spirit with mousy-brown hair.

Her name is Julie. Well, truthfully, I don't remember her name. It ended with an "e" sound. Tammy, Wendy, Lori? Let's go with Julie.

We met at a family-friendly spiritual conference that gathered each summer at a different college campus. We both volunteered to work with kids to help pay the costs and connected during a short break on a bench under a large oak over talk of kids.

"How old is yours?" I asked with a nod toward her son. He was a very tall four-year-old. A year younger than my daughter.

They lived on the east coast; I was then

living in the Midwest. Neither of us had been to this conference before.

"How's the week going for you and for your family?"

"How do you like the workshop you are taking?"

Questions asked of many at this conference. Answers that no longer matter. Fine. Everything was fine.

Later in the week, we find the same shaded bench. I noticed and complimented her on her belt. It's a rainbow-striped cloth strip with brown leather ends. No more than an inch wide.

She blushes and touches the belt with her index finger.

With eyes fixed on the view straight ahead, she thanked me and then quietly asked, "When did you know you were gay?"

This was in the time of few words to describe "not straight." When the focus was on ways of coupling and the clothes you wore instead of ways of being. I can't remember how she knew. A conversation or an assumption based on the fact that I was attending the conference with my gay best friend would be my guess. I remember not feeling surprised by the question.

"I'm not. I date both men and women. For me, it isn't about the parts, it is about the person," I shared. I rearranged myself on the bench, thinking about the people I had been involved with and crushed on, until I noticed a flash of orange as a robin flew overhead. "There was never a moment of not knowing. More of an unwinding realization. It has always felt true even when I was too shy or uncertain to act on it."

"You?"

She blushes again. "After I met my husband. Before we were married."

She takes time to run through her story. "I thought it would pass." "Now, we have our son." She takes another moment to replay decisions made along the way, finally saying, "He's a good father. He's kind."

We sit for a long while, honoring the weight of these newly-spoken words in our silence.

I ran into Julie some years later when the conference was being held in a small university town in Wisconsin. She had a very young child in her arms. Her son was drawing chalk pictures on the sidewalk near them. We stood together watching the drawing come to life. She bounced up and down gently to soothe the baby.

I congratulate her on the new addition to the family and ask what it is like to care for two. She admits that it is tough; her son is not excited about sharing mom's attention with a newborn.

After a pause, she shares that, despite the work, having two children is really a dream come true. "My husband has really leaned in to help," she offers. "A dream come true," she repeats quietly.

I look for Julie every year. There is no sign of the rainbow belt when I do see her in the conference's public spaces: dining halls, quads, and auditoriums. I wonder if she still has the belt in her closet? When I see rainbows for sale, I think of her and the other quiet ones that make choices that break my heart. We no longer speak. Sometimes confidences shared can keep people apart.

25

Avis Barlow

26

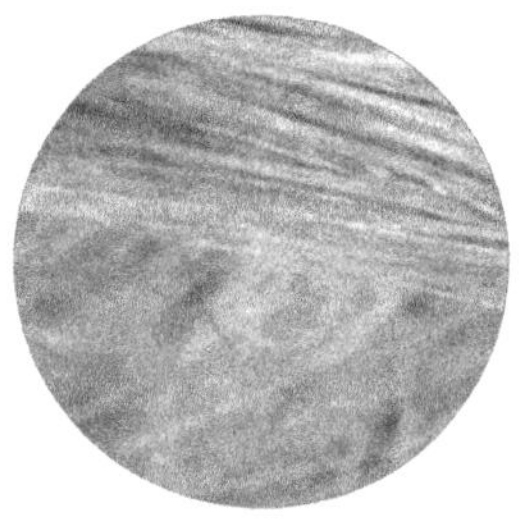

"Many women who cut their hair short after their first baby (and don't like it) swear never to do it again."

Dr. Christina Hibbert [4]

[4] https://www.cosmopolitan.com/style-beauty/beauty/news/a4740/new-postpartum-hairstyle/ accessed 02/16/2024.

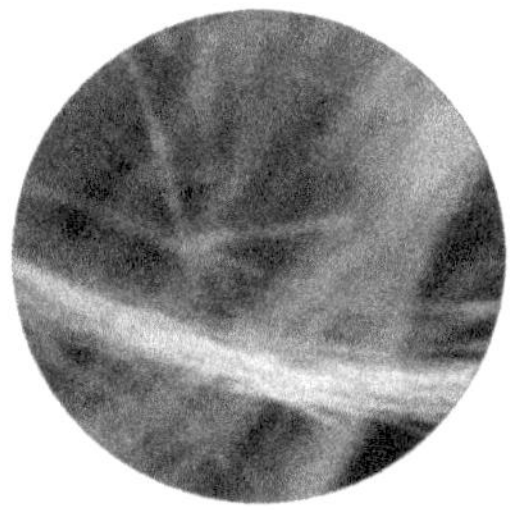

Sign of Affection

Tom worked in the office at a for-profit school for adults looking to improve their lives with a certificate in medical records or by becoming a nursing assistant. He and his marketing executive boyfriend, Roger, my parents, and a friend of my mom's from college and her husband formed a group that would get together for parties.

When it was Tom and Roger's turn to host, Tom took care of the kids at the townhouse they shared near the river. He was the outgoing, silly one of the couple with the bold patterns and easy smile that knew how to talk to kids. He was the adult that checked in on us throughout the night. Our parents were too drunk to care. He endlessly changed the TV channel to make us happy, brought us sodas and colorful bowls of delicious name-brand snacks that we were never allowed because of their price, and made sure we had a good time.

A decade later, single now, he was the gay uncle that made me strong drinks at the bottom-rung gay tavern in town. The one with the tiny dance floor and stage. Frequented by aging drag performers; old men slouched on their stools looking at boys in too-tight clothes that were looking for money, and college students of all flavors there for the cheap drinks. He was less bold and sparkly, but still had a knack for making sure that we all had fun and got home safely.

Tom's story ended in middle age when he was killed in a downtown park. After bartime just before dawn. Near a public bathroom that was known within the community as a place to go when you were looking for casual sex with other men.

The murderer's story was very different. He claimed he was a hunter that came to the park to shoot rabbit. In camouflaged clothes with a gun. Downtown. In the middle of the night.

This was not classified as a hate crime. Nor is it easy to find reference to it then or now. The killer's name and whether he is a free man remain hidden. I wonder if he still hunts.

32

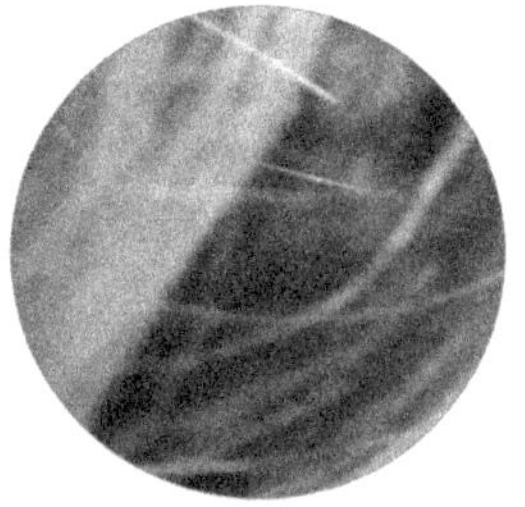

Rabbits have very thin and delicate skin that is covered with fine fur comprised of both a soft undercoat and stiff guard hairs. Care must be taken when clipping fur because the skin is prone to tearing." [5]

[5] https://www.ncbi.nlm.nih.gov/pmc/articles/PMC7152457 accessed 02/16/2024.

Avis Barlow

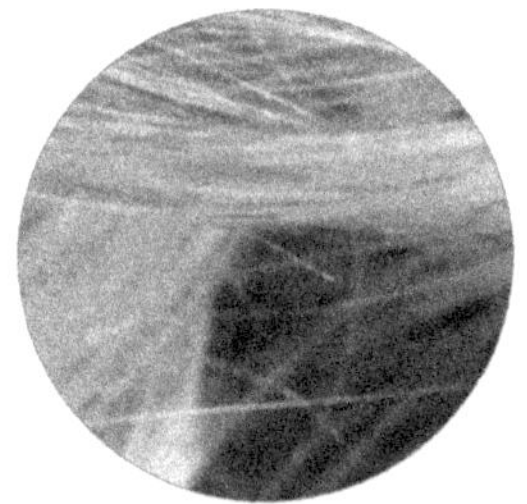

Testicular

I've been told that bodies with testicles prefer short styles and young bodies with ovaries require long hair. Older bodies with ovaries have less value and so fewer rules.

When my daughter was eight, she tried a short haircut, bangs, and a fedora hat. She loved herself hard and leaned fully into her style. That summer, we went on a family trip that included a visit to a children's museum she loved, where kids could pretend to work in a grocery store and be television reporters, doctors, and nurses, and the like.

While we were playing patient and doctor in a fake ambulance, another mom pointed at Ricki, as she was known then, and referred to her as a "little boy" when telling her son to wait his turn. She did it again when she explained the reason for the green screen behind that little boy from the ambulance; my daughter.

When she was born, she was bald. Not even eyebrows. The baby photographer from the mall that recorded the three-, six-, and 9-month milestones felt it important that we include a pink hat and pink feather boa over her pink outfit. Lest we be confused or unsure. Visually inviting us to pray that the preferred hairstyle for bodies with ovaries flows to her, too.

Now, she's a young adult figuring out her way forward in a world where she has been hassled by grown men since she was 13. Men followed her in the grocery store in middle school and rubbed up against her on the train when she traveled to high school. Now, there is always someone trying to ask her out or to get her number. She is rarely seen by men as a whole person with value beyond her looks nor is she ever really safe.

She went nearly a decade without cutting her hair after that incident at the children's museum. Now, when she's going out, she straightens out the natural wave in her long hair. The baby photographer would be so pleased.

Corpus Memoria: Hair

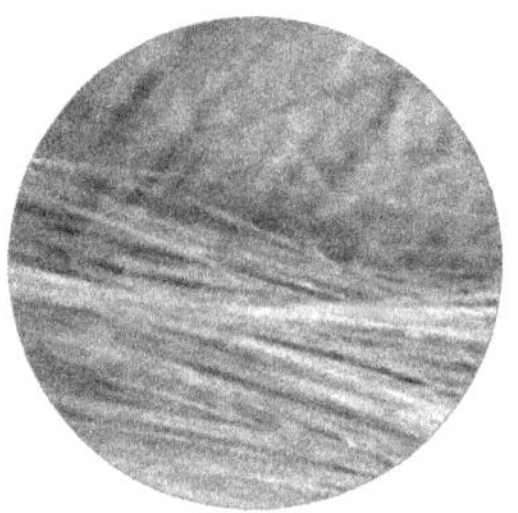

Lanugo is a baby's first hair. It helps protect a fetus' skin from being damaged by amniotic fluid and regulates their temperature until they develop enough body fat. The hairs also help a fetus grow by sending vibrations that stimulate growth when it moves.

Once lanugo is shed, typically in the last eight weeks of gestation, it mixes with amniotic fluid which the fetus swallows in utero. The tiny hairs are passed in their first poop at birth. [6]

[6] https://my.clevelandclinic.org/health/body/22487-lanugo accessed 02/16/2024.

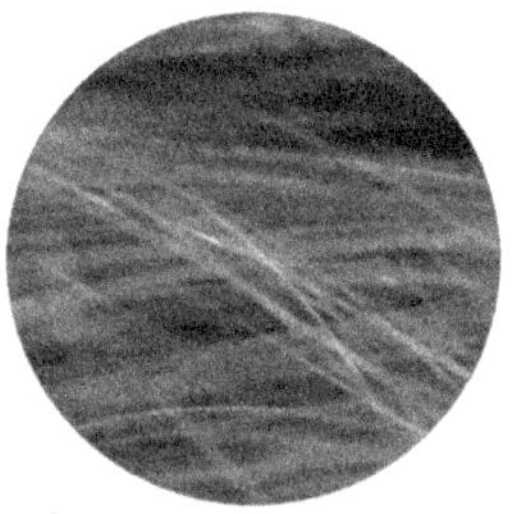

Real

Frank, with the mischief in his eyes and sweet lips, was a quietly butch gay friend in my world of New York piano bar queens. He was the quiet one among the showy folk. He ignored their lack of interest in him and their constant wondering about why his partner of 30 years kept him around. They are so different, everyone said.

Frank was small, dark-skinned and wore black jeans and leather wherever we went. A collared shirt, maybe if it was fancy. But, when you think of Frank, it is his dry wit and understated stories of great travel adventures that you remember. No small talk. I always felt deeply seen.

While the rest of them talked of musicals, singers, reviews, gossip, and upcoming shows, Frank and I talked of travels, sports, and life. First in the piano bar, later over football games and get-togethers. I last saw him when I was living in Washington, DC. He came down from New York for the big march on the capital for lesbian, gay, and bi equality. During the weekend, we planned camping trips that no longer than made sense. He was already being killed from the inside out by the disease that boiled the flesh and juice from much of my generation of gay friends.

I had left for another city when Frank finally died: angry at his loss of dreams and travels until the end. There was no surrender. I was in school and too broke to travel back for his memorial service, so I sent something to be read. His partner sent me a small ceramic figure of a smiling black cat standing behind a black box with a strip of sandpaper on the top side meant to hold wooden matches. A possession Frank's family did not claim and his partner didn't want.

It was a strange time when only birth families could attend to next-of-kin tasks. They carelessly or deliberately erased in an instant the lives and loves made and sustained in adulthood. If the family was kind, obituaries of men dying young of unnamed causes listed male "close friends" with the parents and siblings. Parents worry aloud to me that their children are making gender and sexual identity selections in response to some fad fueled by the media. It is these erased and compartmentalized stories that come to mind.

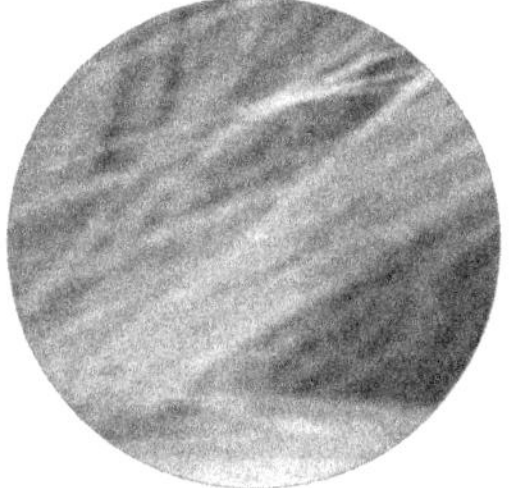

The frequency of hair loss in secondary syphilis ranges from 2.9% to 7%. The hair loss can be moth-eaten, diffuse or both. The "moth-eaten" pattern is the most common type and is considered to be a pathognomonic manifestation of secondary syphilis. The alopecia, which is non-scarring, usually affects the scalp and occasionally the eyebrows, beard, and pubic area. [7]

[7] https://www.ncbi.nlm.nih.gov/pmc/articles/ PMC3537782 accessed 02/24/2024.

46

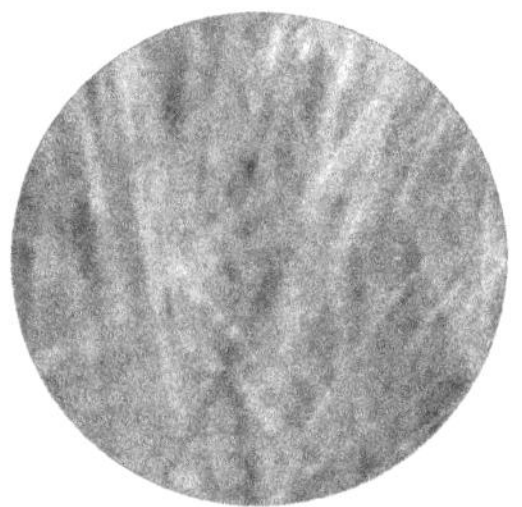

Appearances

I met Juana through a friend. She first worked in the bookstore at the university I attended and then a restaurant and then another place with an easy-to-get job. She was my friend's weed connection on the side. Always something on the side. Butch and confident with her short black hair and shoulders broad and strong in cotton and flannel. She had infinite stories of a bright future that flew against the economies of the present moment. I mouthed the words, "look at me," or, more honestly, "pick me" silently by getting too drunk to walk home, unexpectedly showing up at her apartment, and by calling too much. She kindly sidestepped me and chased volatile femmes of all kinds. Usually a destructive crush with dramatic fighting. Often something on the side.

A few years after we met, she fell hard

for her final femme, Melodia. Their last night together, they broke up and fought hard enough that Ria left for her parents' house. When Juana followed her there, Ria's brother came outside saying, "I'm going to kill you because you're gay and you turned my sister gay." He shot her five or more times in the face and chest, beat her with his gun, and then kicked her motionless body. Not hate, he said. He was afraid for his sister and mother. Despite protests from national LGBTQ groups, the state agreed. The judge disagreed. Her brother is still in prison and feels wronged because of the involvement of those groups with an agenda. I wonder how Ria feels.

49

50

Hairwork jewelry of the early Victorian period (1837-1860) sometimes served as mourning jewelry, made from the hair of and worn to honor a recently departed loved one. People also gave hair brooches or bracelets as a token of love or friendship. Linherr and Company of New York offered a full line of bracelets, brooches, and necklaces made to order from hair supplied by the customer. [8]

[8] https://madcohistory.org/online-exhibits/vintage-jewelry-people-who-wore-it-introduction/jewelry-made-of-hair/ accessed 02/24/2024.

52

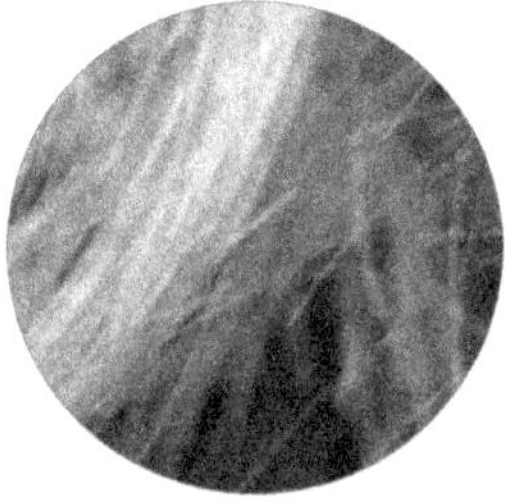

Not Pretty

"I need a haircut." I told the person that answered the phone of the salon closest to my new house. "Today. With someone that has experience cutting curly hair." I was told to come in 45 minutes later to see K.

When I sat in the chair, I met K, an African-American queer hair diva who wore black leggings and skirts like mine and mixed feminine, masculine, and queer style elements in a way that I admired. Three previous stylists wouldn't cut my curly hair shorter than shoulder length: they were concerned that I looked pretty. I needed them to cut every hair my ex had touched. It needed to be gone. "My boy side needs to be seen, not just my girl side," I said. "I am not this person," I said while they played with my hair.

When asked what kind of style I wanted, I pulled out printed pages of Caucasian heads of both genders with different variations of styles featuring both shaved and curly hair: long and short in one style.

An hour later, as K swept up the many many pieces of me that had been dead for a long while, I felt lighter than I had in decades. I ran my hand over the cut, a high fade with long curly bangs, feeling relieved. I thought I was there to wash my ex out of my hair but found out she wasn't the real driver. I needed to speak my gender mix aloud to someone. It was perfect magic that K was chosen to bear witness.

That glimmer of expressed authenticity and being able to see something closer to the me I feel inside when I look in the mirror made me quietly bold enough to get a therapist to start to pluck these parts of me from the shelf and to rejoin the online dating world.

Before moving on, let me quickly share an overview of my sex life up to this point:

     Woman 1
     Woman 2
          Man 1
     Woman 2
          Man 2
          men
     Woman 3
          men
          Man 3 - 5

men

Man 5

men

Man 6

men

Man 7

Man 8

MOTHERHOOD INTERRUPTS

men

Man 9

Woman 4

Note: The length of the gap between Woman 3 and Woman 4 was so long because: lesbians were generally not interested in me unless they were new to it; the bisexual women interested in me were more femme-presenting than I was seeking; and the women I met required more effort and offered more of themselves than I could handle. I had close friends and a life that satisfied all of my needs except sex. Bottom line: men were easier.

Since Man 7, my online dating activity was mostly soaking in the lives of those that shared their profiles and then imagining a life with them much in the same way I shop for kitchen appliances.

After Woman 4 and this haircut, I changed my profile to define who I was seeking with more specificity.

I am attracted to folk in any type of body that are fluid and confident in how their masculine/feminine aspects intersect and present themselves or they reject that shit altogether.

I joined other dating apps only for queer and trans folks and stopped lurking when aligned folks posted. People started seeing me as more queer than straight. I met some wonderful people around the country on virtual dates, dates on vacations, vacations only taken to meet people, dates with tequila, readings, and outdoor blues concerts. Through these encounters, I got to practice showing up now that I had a better sense of myself. I learned how to say "yes" and, for the first time, "no" to dates and sex and relationships aloud.

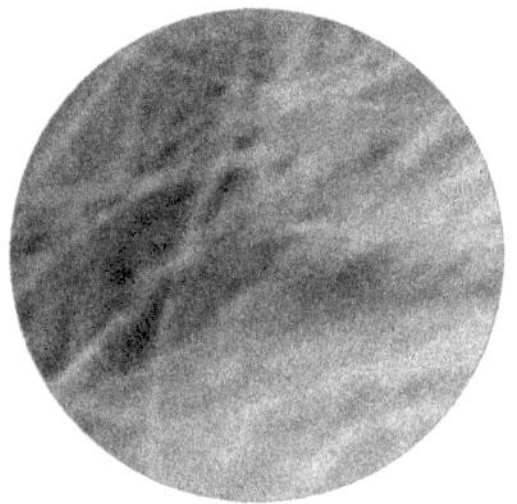

A single one-inch strand of hair can be used to identify one person from among 10 million.

The protein content of that single strand tells you whether it comes from a person's head, arm, or pubic area, helpful for forensic identification. [9]

[9] https://www.llnl.gov/article/45421/llnl-led-study-finds-any-single-hair-human-body-can-be-used-identification# accessed 02/24/2024.

Things I Don't Want My Phone To Know [10]

There are things I don't want my phone to know. Things I can barely admit to myself. Writing them down comes with a dryness that grips the sides of my throat and fills my mouth with metal.

I can't tell my phone about our first time together after a year of mostly texts and a few calls. How the hypotheticals and the realities of our meeting crashed together. My phone is curious but knows something is wrong. It offers soothing videos.

I can't ask my phone if I should bother to respond to the two let's-just-be-friends sentences you typed into your phone months later.

My phone won't know if we've reached

[10] An earlier version of this story appears in the anthology, Places Like Home, edited by Ariel Gore. Published by The Literary Kitchen in March 2020.

that moment when you ask, "How was it for you?" Only wanting to hear "fine" or "good" instead of "confusing" or "shameful." Honestly, neither will I.

I can't tell my phone how I felt when you pressed your forearm down on my throat and rough-handled my breasts. How my mind engaged and my body puffed and surrendered for one or two seconds with desire.

If I think about this too loudly, my phone will have suggestions I don't want others to see.

I can't tell you about the softness of your mouth or the taste of your sex. How your fingers stroking my genitals made me feel right in this body for the first time with another body. Nor can I admit how scary all that is to remember. My phone knows I underestimate firsts. It judges me for that.

I can't tell my phone that I have little experience surrendering and saying no. That I leave my body. That the eighteen-year-old anxious boy that talks too fast or the porn star that takes over—excited, obnoxious, and unsteady—are just characters that offer false protection.

My phone is unqualified to diagnose me or call for help. It's not able to fully consider the realms of human consciousness under stressful conditions.

I can't tell my phone of the persistent shame in my chest because I couldn't hear your body and care for you in the way I'd looked forward to many times.

It's too painful to share.

I can't ask my phone how to make amends for trying to get you to agree to a speculative, but perfect, future together so relentlessly that it made you take a giant step back. My phone would applaud my attempts at persuasion and offer tips to do better next time, completely missing the point.

I can't tell my phone that I have warm affection for you. It might tell you. One of you will surely laugh.

I can't ask my phone about my fears or how to deepen connections from a distance. It would list couples therapist names. We aren't a couple. That reminder would make me sad.

Instead, I watch our curiosity and affection transform with time into a smoke that deadens feelings and makes us polite.

Still, I can't tell my phone to say goodbye.

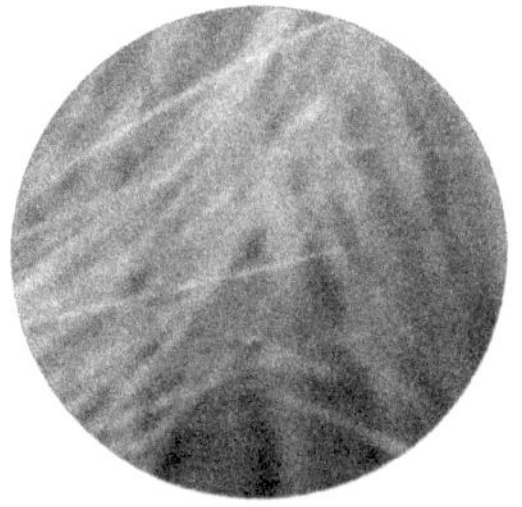

A case of hair loss has been reported over the temporal region of the skull from repeated, prolonged conversations on a mobile phone. Biopsy is negative for any other pathology of hair loss. Limiting the duration of mobile phone usage and having a hands-free cord to keep the mobile phone away from the ear, in addition to more common hair-loss treatments, helped in hair regrowth. [11]

[11] https://www.researchgate.net/publication/312218192_Hair_Loss_due_to_Electromagnetic_Radiation_from_Overuse_of_Cell_Phone 02/24/2024..

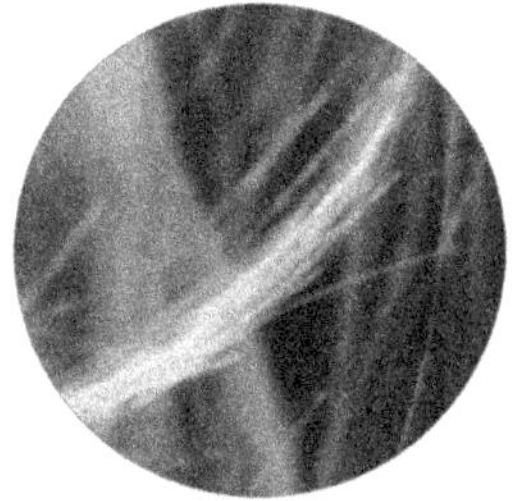

Unexpected

I was married this past weekend. It was a small affair in a public garden surrounded by an old forest that welcomed us loudly when we first visited in the rainy autumn and, later, when we stood before our beloved community on our specially chosen warm summer day.

I suppose I should back up a few years. To a personal ad written a few months before a national quarantine on a queer dating site where you post short ads instead of images. It was written by a trans nonbinary queer in Boston looking for a masculine-of-center (MOC) trans guy for a warm connection and hot nights. It piqued my interest but included the writer's Hogwarts house (Gryffindor) and I was sure that they played quidditch on the weekend. Also, I am not a guy and had turned queers off in the recent past when I wore a skirt instead of pants on first dates.

Z's second ad came at the beginning of pandemic quarantine at the cajoling of a friend who advised them to not take the lack of response to the first ad to heart. He gave it one more try.

> Hard Times to find something magical. Let's find the unexpected connection. Are you out there being proper and good? Imagining more improper activities? MOC for MOC or nonbinary, looking for a spark.

No Potter reference and the net opened to nonbinary folk which, even though I wore skirts, felt like it included me.

> Hi Z. I just got done buying two new sex toys so maybe not quite as good and proper as you seek.

> I'm sheltering in Atlanta. Nonbinary fluid human. Like looking things up for fun. New ideas are very very shiny to me. So are new possibilities.

For two days, we texted in the dating app, ascertained that we had a person we knew in common (very important in queer circles for safety), checked each other out via social media, and liked what we saw. After confirming that there was indeed a spark, we exchanged phone numbers.

Three days later, we had our first virtual date. We were both nervous and drank brown liquor for courage. The date lasted for hours. We asked each other a lot of questions. Some were silly, like favorite soup, and some deeper like gender, family, traumatic experiences, and what were our flaws. We led with our worst traits, qualities, and actions. Daring the other one to back away and, with the possibility of death hanging closer than usual, we were cutting to the chase. Better to know we weren't a fit than not. At one point, Z informed me that the people he chose fell into two categories: Tricks or Spouses. Whenever I would try to take us down a sexy flirty path, he would pull it back to something deeper. I fell into the Spouse category; he knew it and named it right away.

After our second or third virtual date, I calculated the distance between our houses and found the midpoint, Shenandoah, Virginia, and suggested an in-person rendezvous for the summer solstice. It was the early days of the pandemic and the idea of this meet-cute moment felt extremely unsafe to those around us. Leaving the house, meeting a stranger out of state, at a cabin in the woods no less, and traveling when we had been advised to shelter in place. People were dying and there was no known cure. My feeling? Whatever was building between us felt like a big deal, but we wouldn't know for sure from afar. In other words, what were we waiting for? Z is a scientist and, after prudently consulting with his scientist friends on the probability of infection, agreed. After going back and forth a bit, we settled on a long weekend at a cabin with a hot tub, good reviews, and a liberal cancellation policy.

Beforehand, we agreed that first-night sex was off the table after an eight-hour drive spent in anticipation of what was to come.

I was the first to arrive. A quick tour revealed a homy place with a ceramic goose in almost every room. After a very fidgety hour of waiting and strategically arranging myself to appear casual and at ease, Z arrived. I was at the table pretending to write when they opened the screen door and walked in with their stuff. Neither of us knew what to do with our bodies. Only our hearts and minds had met. I covered it by giving them a long, confident hug.

That night, we ate, spent time in the hot tub, Z read an erotic story they had published, and we made out until our mouths had a shared language to communicate our desire. Then, once our bodies felt their way to safety, we slept.

The rest of the weekend was spent visiting caves and mountaintops, hanging out in the hot tub, and practicing a new-to-me kind of touch that listens to the waves of energy building and crashing as often as possible, exploration with explicit consent, instead of bearing down toward release. And we slept.

"The dumbest thing I've ever done is drive in the opposite direction of you," he texted before getting on the freeway.

After six months of alternating three-week dates at each other's places, we took a trip to Portland, Oregon and affirmed that we were being called to a life together there and made it so.

A little over a year later, Z proposed with an illustrated book of flowers with meaning connected to our journey. He thwarted all my efforts to micromanage the moment by presenting it on my birthday. To make sure I knew that he enthusiastically chose me. I said yes and then, in an unfortunate moment of speaking all of the interior things that should never be shared, questioned whether he really planned to propose that particular weekend, inferring that it was haphazardly last-minute versus thoughtfully planned. The fact that he stays with me when I react so poorly to unmanipulated displays of affection is the bigger testimony to our love.

Raised in a world that prohibited our marriage for most of our lives fueled our desire for that garden celebration. It pushed us on even as we navigated the unpleasantly gendered path to figure out what outfit would best align our inner selves with the image that others would see. Unlike the other details, like the flowers, the imagery on our rings, and the design of the marriage certificate that all gathered would sign in witness to our union, this detail was deflating.

That Friday morning, after shopping for a t-shirt for Z and taking diuretics to make sure my ridiculous platform gladiator sandals would fit my feet, we went to the county records office to pick up the paperwork. Folks were waiting either for tax records or marriage documents, it was easy to spot which records people needed. As we waited, I thought about my friends, Mark and Michael, and other queer couples who got married quickly at the courthouse before politicians changed their minds and made what was legal, somehow not.

The days before the ceremony and the weekend after was a coming together of different groups into one beloved circle that surrounded our family. There was an ease and a graciousness to our helpful clan, a blessing to our new life in our new city, that was exactly what Z and I imagined. We didn't share our vows with one another before that moment in the circle under the trees. Once there, we both declared, "I choose you."

A guest that I've known since childhood came out during our wedding weekend as a late-in-life gay explorer. Our friends thought to get nosy because he was wearing a rainbow bracelet and he felt free to share that part of himself with a group so at home with who they are. That he felt easy sharing that part of himself made all the gathered queers warm-hearted in their gossip.

That week, the wedding, and the day-to-day of this relationship is an unexpected joy savored in a world of hate.

Avis Barlow

Acknowledgments

The writing group at Charis Books and More, hosted by ER Anderson, that first gave me courage and inspiration to begin to write with the intention of sharing beyond my journal. AFM SNG for a chance to dig into writing and community on a regular basis.

My ride-or-die believing-mirrors, healers, and cheerleaders: Robin, Kelsey, Juniper, Laura, Hannah, Mark, Greg, David, Paige, Sandy, Michell, Todd, Ian, Virginia, Anna, Elisa, Tricia, Sue, and Lauren.

The teachers and workshop leaders who shared their wisdom, edits, inspiration, and a glimpse into the writer's life. Most especially: Ariel Gore, Chelsey Clammer, Cooper Lee Bombardier, Megan Milks, and Andrea Lawler.

The Wayward Writers, Mavens of Mythmaking, and writers of the Literary Kitchen for their insightful feedback and supportive community. Special shoutout to Dusty Bryndal and Christa Orth for holding me accountable and holding my hand.

Mom, Jill, Dan, Jason, Dawn, Jared, Mike, and Michael for the stories, love, and acceptance.

Merrick and Zane, for all the things.

Avis Barlow

Avis Barlow delights in telling stories that privilege the warped and juicy moments of life. This collection is part of a larger work-in-progress that uses body parts to remember life stories. When not writing, Avis looks up things for fun and speaks truth to their dog and anyone else that will listen. They live in Portland, Oregon.

Claire Dierksen spends time as a graphic designer, potter, and body worker. She is a portal of big thoughts and big pots. She currently lives all over the PNW.

—

10% of the profits of this book will be donated to charities serving the needs of the LGBTQIA2+ community.
Queer lives matter.